RETURN FROM
PLANET
VIDA

David Ellis Grey

To order additional copies of this book, contact:
Xlibris
844-714-8691
www.Xlibris.com
Orders@Xlibris.com

ISBN: Softcover   978-1-6698-7331-0
        EBook   978-1-6698-7332-7

Print information available on the last page

Rev. date: 04/05/2023

"This sequel to Exploring Planet VIDA is dedicated to my beautiful grandchildren who I love dearly and support my fun fictional stories. Their interest in reading, and the smile on their face makes it all worthwhile."

One year after shuttle astronauts were unexpectedly thrown off course and accidently bounced into another universe, they finally make it home to Earth.

Doctors quickly arrived and performed a medical check-up to ensure all astronauts are healthy.

The astronauts joyfully reunite
with their family and friends.

Local newspapers and TV stations as well as government officials arrived to interview the astronauts to discussed their journey, and ask many questions, including why they were unable to communicate with the astronauts for almost a year! They were also curious about the unusual and strange looking shuttle craft they returned to earth in.

The people of earth were unaware of the astronaut's exploration of Planet VIDA and wanted to know more details about their visit.

So, the crew held a meeting inviting everyone to a huge townhall with news media from around the world to hear about their adventure into space, and their surprising discovery of Planet VIDA. A presentation with photos and video clips of Planet VIDA are shared with everyone in attendance.

The astronauts explained how a piece of floating space debris unexpectedly hit their shuttle, throwing them off course into another galaxy and forcing them to crash-land onto this unknown Earth-like planet.

Local townspeople and the media were very surprised to hear of other life in the universe! They were also surprised to hear that life on planet VIDA was very similar to Earth.

The crew explained how friendly and helpful the people of Planet VIDA were. They also explained how the planet's limited resources sustained them for survival. Unlike Earth, planet VIDA only had solar and wind to power their transportation, homes, and businesses.

People and animals lived together in unity. All food was grown from the ground. Water from lakes and oceans was always pure enough to drink.

People of Earth wanted to learn more. So, they decided to form a committee of engineers and scientists to determine if a voyage to Planet VIDA was even possible for anyone who wanted to go.

There were many volunteers. Plans were slowly coming together to travel and explore Planet VIDA.

Suddenly, a strange radio signal was detected from outer space. This went on for several days as many people tried to determine where it was coming from.

They later determined the communication signal was very similar to the space shuttle that crash-landed on Planet VIDA over a year ago. "How is this possible?" they asked.

The signal became a little stronger every day. Could it possibly be an unknown space craft traveling closer and closer to Earth? The people of Earth believed it was some form of space craft floating in Earth's atmosphere.

Engineers and Scientists listened and tried to communicate with this possible unknown spacecraft! But after several days the communication signal slowly began to fade.

Eventually, all communication was lost. Earth continues to try and reestablish communication with this unknown space craft every day.

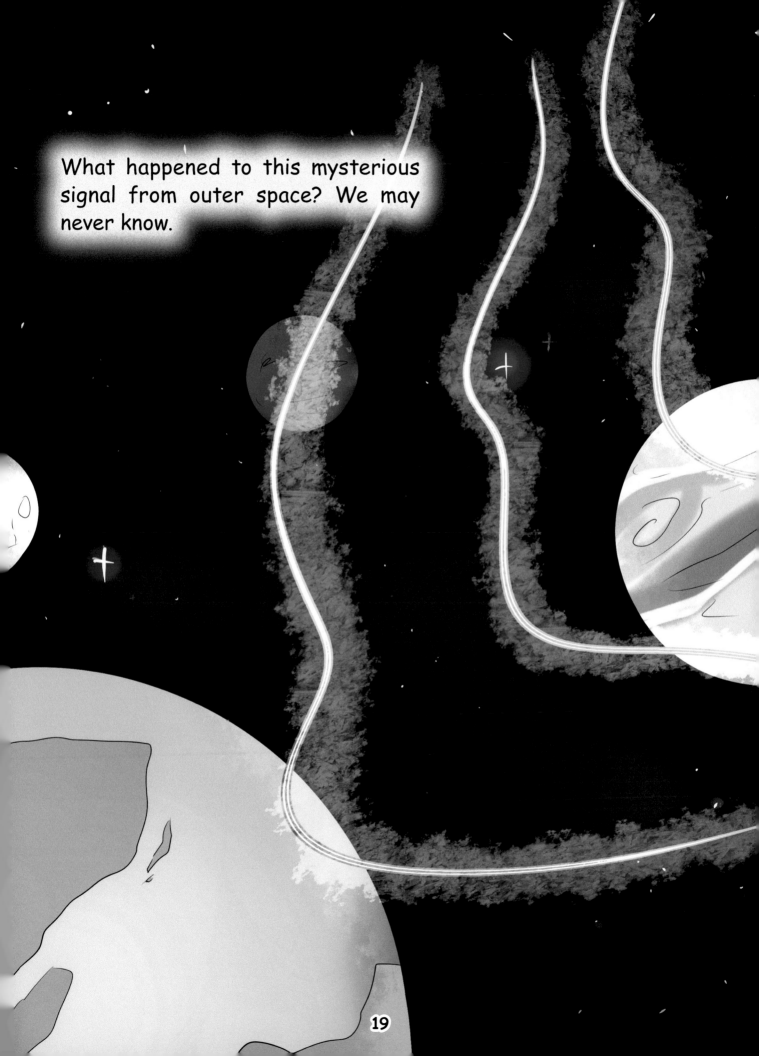

What happened to this mysterious signal from outer space? We may never know.

Printed in the United States
by Baker & Taylor Publisher Services